Phonics Reading Program

HELLO KITTY®

Book 8
long e —
ea

Y0-BCM-028

Squeaky Sneaky

by Quinlan B. Lee
Illustrated by Sachiho Hino

ISBN 978-0-545-47684-3
Text and illustrations © 2007 SANRIO CO., LTD. USED UNDER LICENSE.
Character © 1976 SANRIO CO., LTD. USED UNDER LICENSE.

12 11 10 9 8 7 6 5   14 15 16 17/0
Printed in China   95
First printing, September 2012
Designed by Angela Jun

SCHOLASTIC INC.
New York Toronto London Auckland
Sydney Mexico City New Delhi Hong Kong

Hello Kitty wants to make **treats**.
Mama will **teach** her.
They will make a **feast** of **treats**.

Her friends want to make **treats**, too.
Mama will **teach** them, too.
Then they will all get to **eat** the **feast**!

First, Mama says to **heat** the oven.
Then mix it up!
Then **knead** it out.
Heat, mix, **knead**!
What's next?

Clean up!
Clean up until it is nice and **neat**.
Good! Now it is time to **eat** the **treats**.

Uh-oh! Where are
the **treats**?
Who would **sneak** a
taste of the **treats**?

Hmm . . . do you hear a **squeak**?
Squeak, **squeak**, **squeak**.
Could it be the **sneak** with the **treats**?

There is the **sneak**!
Rory **beat** them to
the **treats**.
Now there will be
no **feast**.

Wait! Mama has more
treats.
It is time to **eat**.
Even the **squeaky
sneak** can **eat!**